Bear's Busy Year

A Book About Seasons

BY MARCIA LEONARD
PICTURES BY BARI WEISSMAN

Troll Associates

Library of Congress Cataloging-in-Publication Data

Leonard, Marcia.
    Bear's busy year: a book about seasons / by Marcia Leonard;
    pictures by Bari Weissman.
        p.   cm.
        Summary: A young bear enjoys being outside during all four
seasons, whether he is playing in the spring rain, wading in his
pool in the summer, picking pumpkins in the fall, or sledding in the
winter.
        ISBN 0-8167-1720-6 (lib. bdg.)   ISBN 0-8167-1721-4 (pbk.)
        [1. Seasons—Fiction.   2. Bears—Fiction.]   I. Weissman, Bari,
ill.   II. Title.
PZ7.L549Bc   1990
[E]—dc20   89-4946

Once there was a bear who was always busy.

In all four seasons, in all kinds of weather,
he liked to be outside doing something.

In spring, when the sky was rainy and gray,
the bear put on a raincoat, a rain hat,
and a pair of red boots.

Then he hurried outside to splash in the puddles and squish in the mud.

And when the rain clouds blew away, he went out into the garden to look at all the green, growing things.

In summer, when the sun was hot and bright,
the bear put on a T-shirt and shorts,
sandals and sunglasses.

Then he raced outside to build a
city in his sandbox.

And when the days grew very hot and muggy,
he ran through the sprinkler
and waded in his pool.

In fall, when the air turned cool and crisp,
the bear put on a flannel shirt,
corduroy pants, and a jacket.

Then he skipped outside
to help his parents pick
apples and pumpkins and squash.

And when the wind whooshed through the trees,
he played tag with the falling leaves.

In winter, when frost made patterns on the window,
the bear put on a snowsuit and boots,
a stocking cap and mittens.

Then he rushed outside to catch the
first flakes of snow.

And when the snow was deep on the ground,
he went sledding with his friends.

In all four seasons, in all kinds of weather,
the little bear liked to be outside.
But sometimes in winter,
when the air was very cold and the days
were very short, he stayed inside.

Then he curled up in his favorite chair
and thought about all the wonderful things
he could do when the next busy year began.